P9-APC-582

Stories for Boys

Stories for Boys

tiger tales®

Contents

I'm Not Going Out There!

by Paul Bright Illustrated by Ben Cort

I'm underneath the bed,
Hardly poking out my head.
It's a squeeze and hurts my knees,
but I don't care.
Can you guess, do you know,
Why I whisper soft and low?

I'M NOT GOING OUT THERE!

There's a dragon breathing smoke,
Who looks far too fierce to stroke,
And his eyes have a scary sort of stare.
I hope he doesn't stay,
But he's not what makes me say,

I'M NOT GOING OUT THERE!

There's a ghost who has no head,
With some toast and chocolate spread,
Which I'm sure he would be very
pleased to share.
And though I'd like a bite,
Still I'm keeping out of sight.
I'M
NOT
GOING
OUT
THERE!

12
9
3
6

There are witches, old and stubbly,
Around a bath all hot and bubbly,
Busy washing all their dirty underwear,
Hanging knickers out to dry,
But they're not the reason why

I'M NOT GOING OUT THERE!

There are monsters of all sizes,
Doing ballet exercises,
Wearing tutus, with pink ribbons in their hair.
And though they look quite charming,
There is something else alarming.

I'M NOT GOING

OUT THERE!

Then there's suddenly a shrieking
And a squealing and a squeaking,
Loud enough to give the boldest beast
a scare.
Now I'm shaking and I'm quaking,
There's a noise of something breaking.

I'M NOT GOING OUT THERE!

The dragon turns quite pale,
From his nostrils to his tail,
Feels a trembling in his tum:
"Oh, I really want my mom!"
"Mustn't panic!" gasps the ghost.
"Keep your head! Don't lose your toast!
I can haunt some other day,
Now I need to get away!"

The witches spill their washing
And go splishing, splashing, sploshing,
Soaked and soapy, slipping, sliding,
Searching for a place to hide in.
Hide from what? They'll soon find out!
They can hear it scream and shout,
And it doesn't sound like fun.
Better hurry! Better run!

The monsters don't feel brave,
But they know how to behave,
So they dance off in a row,
Each one on his tippy-toe.

Then all that I can hear,
Very loud and very near,
Is the thing that made them flee.
Do you know what it could be?

It has teeth that can gnash,
It has eyes that can flash,
I can hear it grumping, jumping,
Hear it stamping, stomping, thumping.
It has hands that can snatch,
It has nails that can scratch.
And it's ready for a fight,
So we're squeezed and
squashed up tight!

There it is—my sister Kate!
And she's in a frightful state,
Making shrieking sounds
and leaping in the air.
By now she must know who
Put the spider in her shoe . . .

. . . I'M NOT GOING OUT THERE!

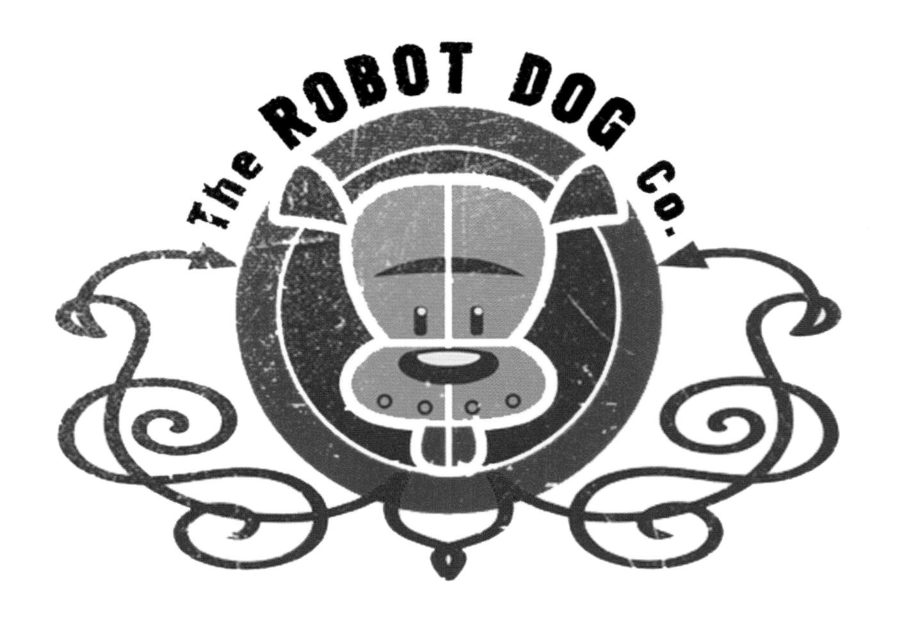
The ROBOT DOG Co.

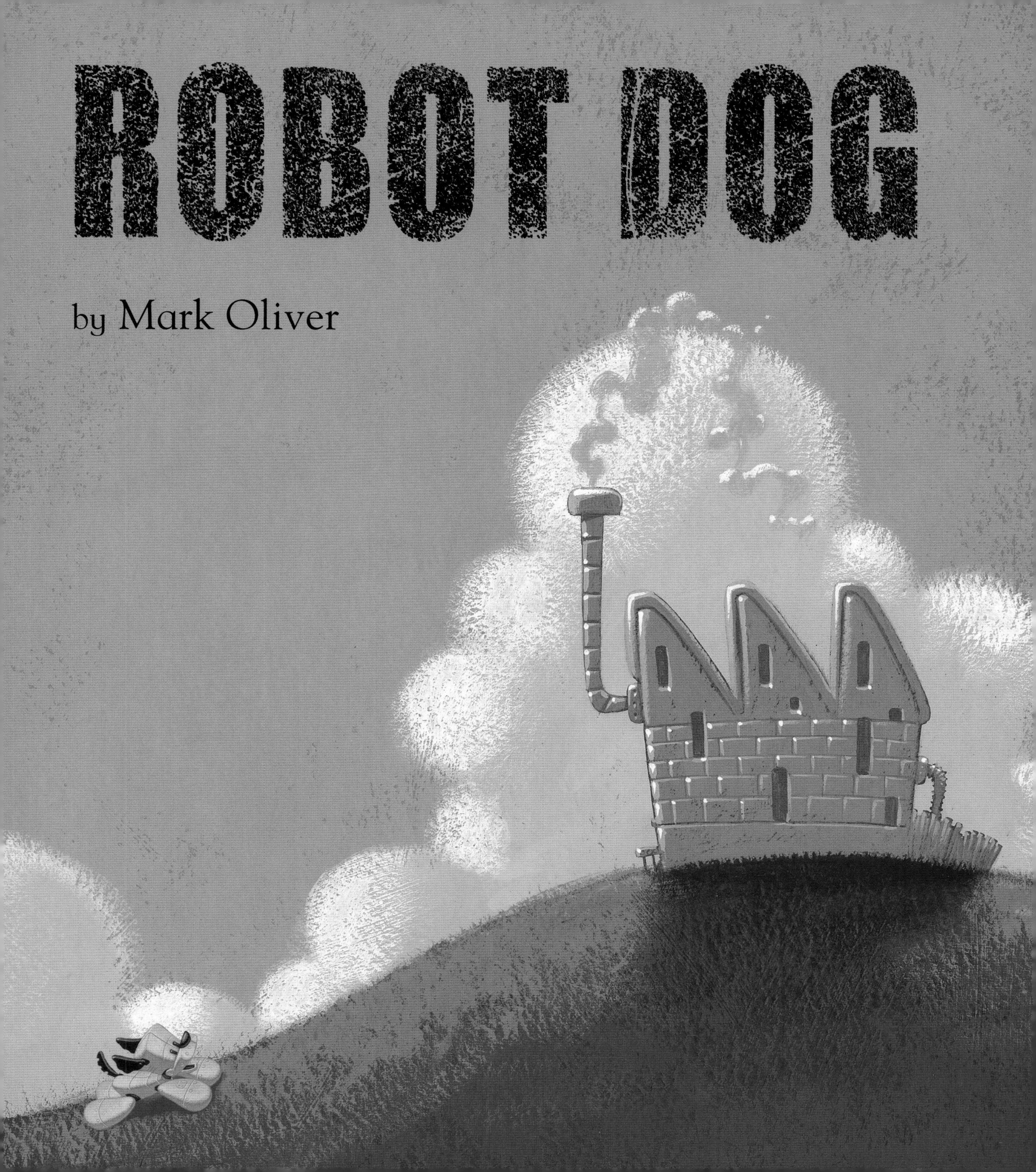
ROBOT DOG
by Mark Oliver

In a factory on a hill,
a huge machine made
robot dogs.

D #2302
D #2301

The robot dogs rolled out of the factory and were delivered to owners who played with them and loved them and cared for them.

The dogs were very happy, because all dogs, even robot dogs, want an owner.

One little dog on the conveyor belt was very excited.

"I wonder what my owner will be like," he said. "What will I be named?"

He was much too excited to sit still—he jumped and frolicked and bounced up and down. But then,

CRASH!

he bounced too high and bumped his ear. At once alarm bells rang, red lights flashed, and a cloud of smoke whooshed as the huge machine ground slowly to a stop.

2304

The machine inspected the robot dog very carefully. Finally a voice boomed:

"NOT RUSTY OR DUSTY,
NOT BATTERED OR BENT,
NO PATCHES OR SCRATCHES,
BUT THERE IS A DENT!
SCRAP!"

So that's my name! thought Scrap as the machine picked him up and dropped him through a hatch.

Scrap slid down a chute and landed in a yard full of junk.

There, staring at him, were some other dogs.

"Hello!" he said. "I'm Scrap! Where am I? Where's my owner?"

One of the dogs said, "You don't have an owner—you're a misfit, like us."

Bumper, Dent, Scratch, and Sniffer all lived in the junkyard. They made it comfortable, and it was a wonderful place to play, just a bit messy—the way dogs like it.

They often played with other dogs who had owners. But sooner or later the other dogs' owners would call:

"Come on, Shiny!"
"Dinnertime, Sparkle!"

Then the other dogs stopped whatever they were doing and ran home.

Seeing the other dogs go off happily to their owners made the yard dogs feel sad.

"Why don't we get an owner?" said Scrap one day.

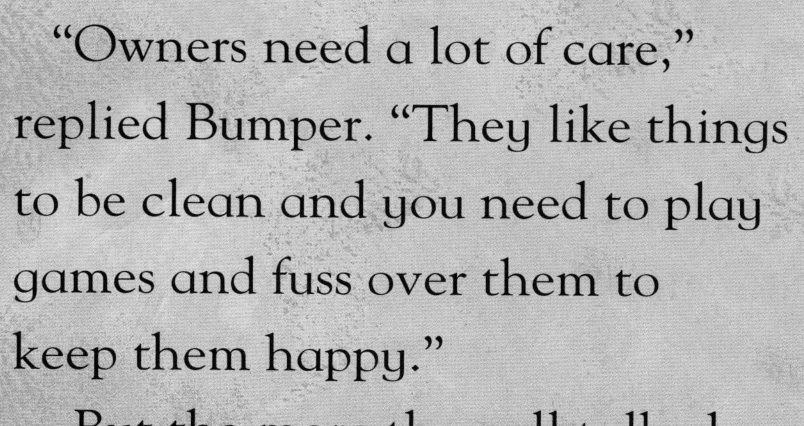

"Owners need a lot of care," replied Bumper. "They like things to be clean and you need to play games and fuss over them to keep them happy."

But the more they all talked about it, the more they really wanted an owner.

"How can we get one?" said Sniffer. "We're misfits!"

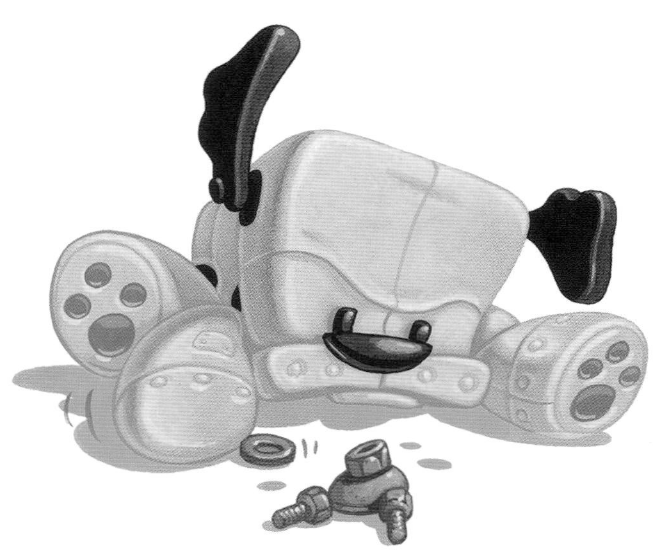

There must be a way, thought Scrap.

As Scrap started thinking, the cogs in his brain started turning. They went around faster and faster as he thought harder and harder.

Finally, a light flickered on!

"I have an idea!" Scrap announced to the other dogs excitedly. "Come help me!"

The dogs raced around collecting anything that might be useful.

They worked all day and all night, and by the next morning the dogs were exhausted, but very proud, because . . .

. . . there stood an owner!

He was rusty and dusty, battered and bent, patched, scratched, and covered in dents—but he had a heart of gold.

2

Their owner played with them and loved them and cared for them. And the dogs were very happy, because all dogs, even robot dogs, want an owner.

0000
12

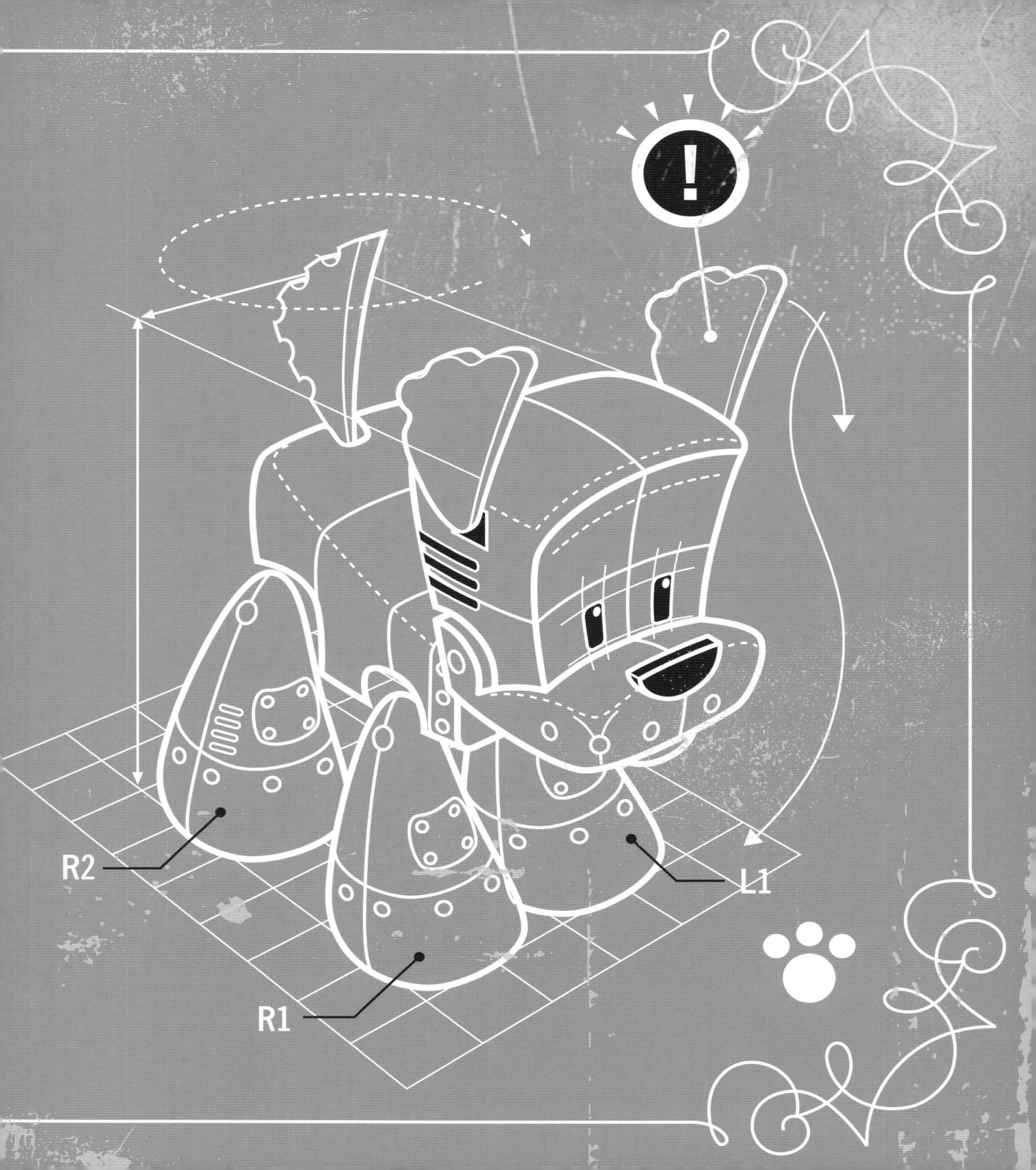
!
R2
R1
L1

Don't Say That, Willy Nilly!

by Anna Powell

Illustrated by
David Roberts

“Willy Nilly,” said his mother, “can you go to the store and buy some cabbage for dinner?”

“**YUK!**” said Willy Nilly.

"Don't say that, Willy Nilly," said his mother. "Say, '**YUM, YUM, WHAT A NICE DINNER!**'"

"Yum, yum, what a nice dinner?" repeated Willy Nilly.

"That's right," said his mother.

"**GOT IT!**" said Willy Nilly.

So Willy Nilly set off to the store.

"YUM, YUM, WHAT A NICE DINNER!
YUM, YUM, WHAT A NICE DINNER!"
repeated Willy Nilly.

Outside the men were emptying trash cans. Willy Nilly said, "Yum, yum, what a nice dinner!"

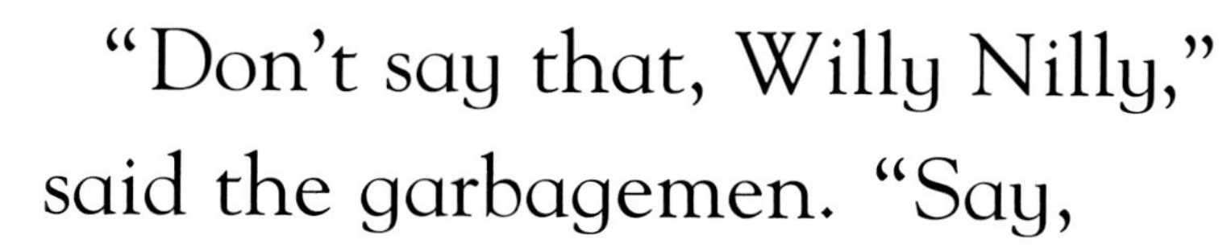

"Don't say that, Willy Nilly," said the garbagemen. "Say, **'GOOD RIDDANCE TO BAD TRASH!'**"

"Good riddance to bad trash?" said Willy Nilly.

"That's right," said the men.

"GOT IT!" said Willy Nilly.

"GOOD RIDDANCE TO BAD TRASH!
GOOD RIDDANCE TO BAD TRASH!"

In the road there was a big moving van. The neighbors were packing up. Willy Nilly said, "Good riddance to bad trash!"

"Don't say that, Willy Nilly," said Mrs. Jones. "Say, '**ENJOY YOUR NEW HOME!**'"

"Enjoy your new home?" said Willy Nilly.

"That's right," said Mrs. Jones.

"**GOT IT!**" said Willy Nilly.

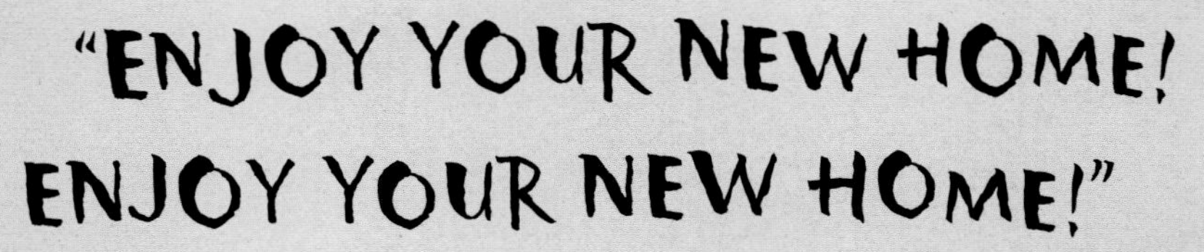

said Willy Nilly as he crossed the park.

The park keeper was picking up some litter from the pond. He began to wobble and . . .

. . . fell into the water with a big

SPLASH!

"Enjoy your new home," said Willy Nilly.

"Don't say that, Willy Nilly," said the park keeper. "Say, '**CAN I HELP YOU OUT OF THERE?**'"

"Can I help you out of there?" said Willy Nilly.

"That's right," said the park keeper.

"**GOT IT!**" said Willy Nilly.

Mr. Thompson's window was open. The parrot looked at Willy Nilly with a beady yellow eye.

"Can I help you out of there?" said Willy Nilly.

"WATCH OUT, I MIGHT BITE!" said the parrot.

"Watch out, I might bite?" said Willy Nilly.

"WATCH OUT, I MIGHT BITE!" said the parrot.

"GOT IT!" said Willy Nilly.

On the sidewalk, Willy met Grandma Macaroon.
"Good morning, Willy Nilly!" said Grandma.
"Watch out, I might bite!" said Willy Nilly.

"Don't say that, Willy Nilly," said Grandma. "Say,

'WHAT A NICE DAY!'"

"What a nice day?" said Willy Nilly.

"That's right," said Grandma.

"GOT IT!" said Willy Nilly.

**"WHAT A NICE DAY!
WHAT A NICE DAY!"**

The window cleaner sped past on his bicycle. He wasn't looking where he was going. He was heading straight into the lamp post.

"What a lovely day!" said Willy Nilly.

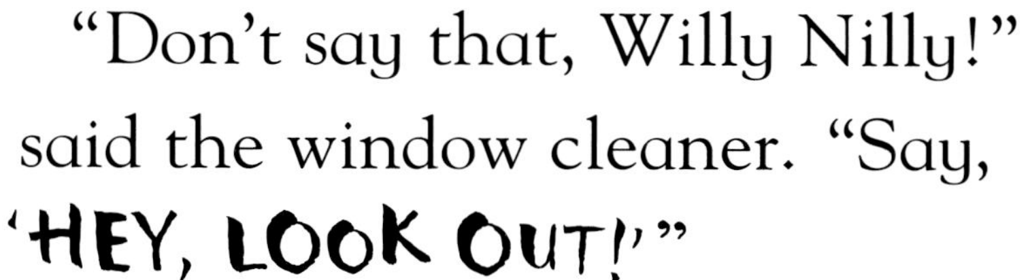

"Don't say that, Willy Nilly!" said the window cleaner. "Say, '**HEY, LOOK OUT!**'"

"Hey, look out?" repeated Willy Nilly.

"That's right," said the window cleaner.

"**GOT IT!**" said Willy Nilly.

In the store, there was a baby in a stroller. Willy Nilly saw the baby reach out to a tower of cans. Oh, no! The cans would fall on top of him.

"**HEY, LOOK OUT!**"
shouted Willy Nilly.

And the baby stopped! Just in time.
"Quick thinking, young man," said the cashier. "What can I do for you?"

"A cabbage, please," said Willy Nilly.

"And what would you like as a thank you?" said the cashier. Willy Nilly chose his favorite thing—ketchup. "Thank you very much," he said.

Willy Nilly went straight home.

"Did you get the cabbage, Willy Nilly?" asked his mother.

"**GOT IT!**" said Willy Nilly.

"Thank you very much," said his mother, and she cooked the cabbage.

Willy Nilly poured ketchup all over his cabbage to make it taste better.

"YUM, YUM, WHAT A NICE DINNER!"

said Willy Nilly.

"YUK!" said his mother.

THE END

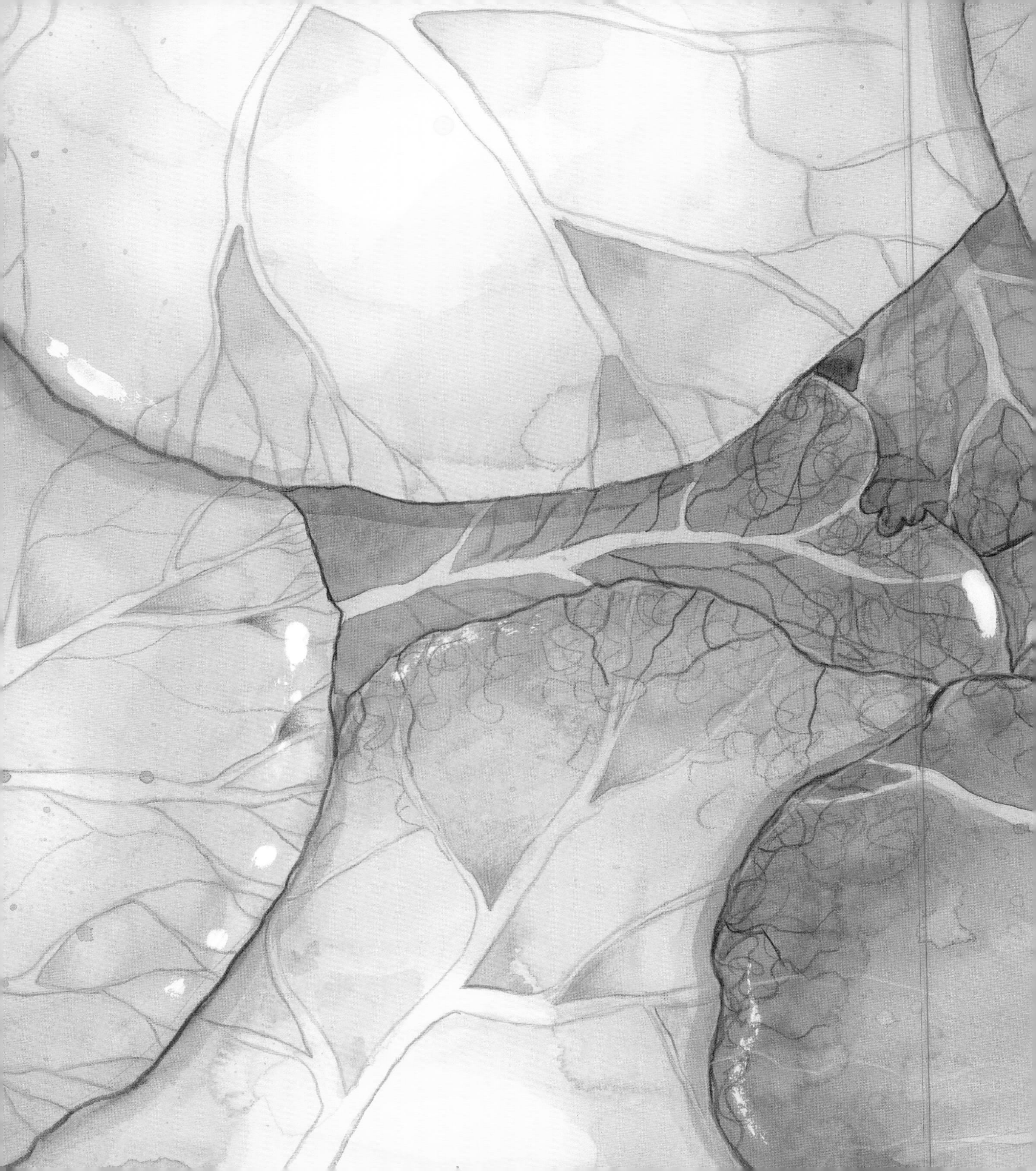

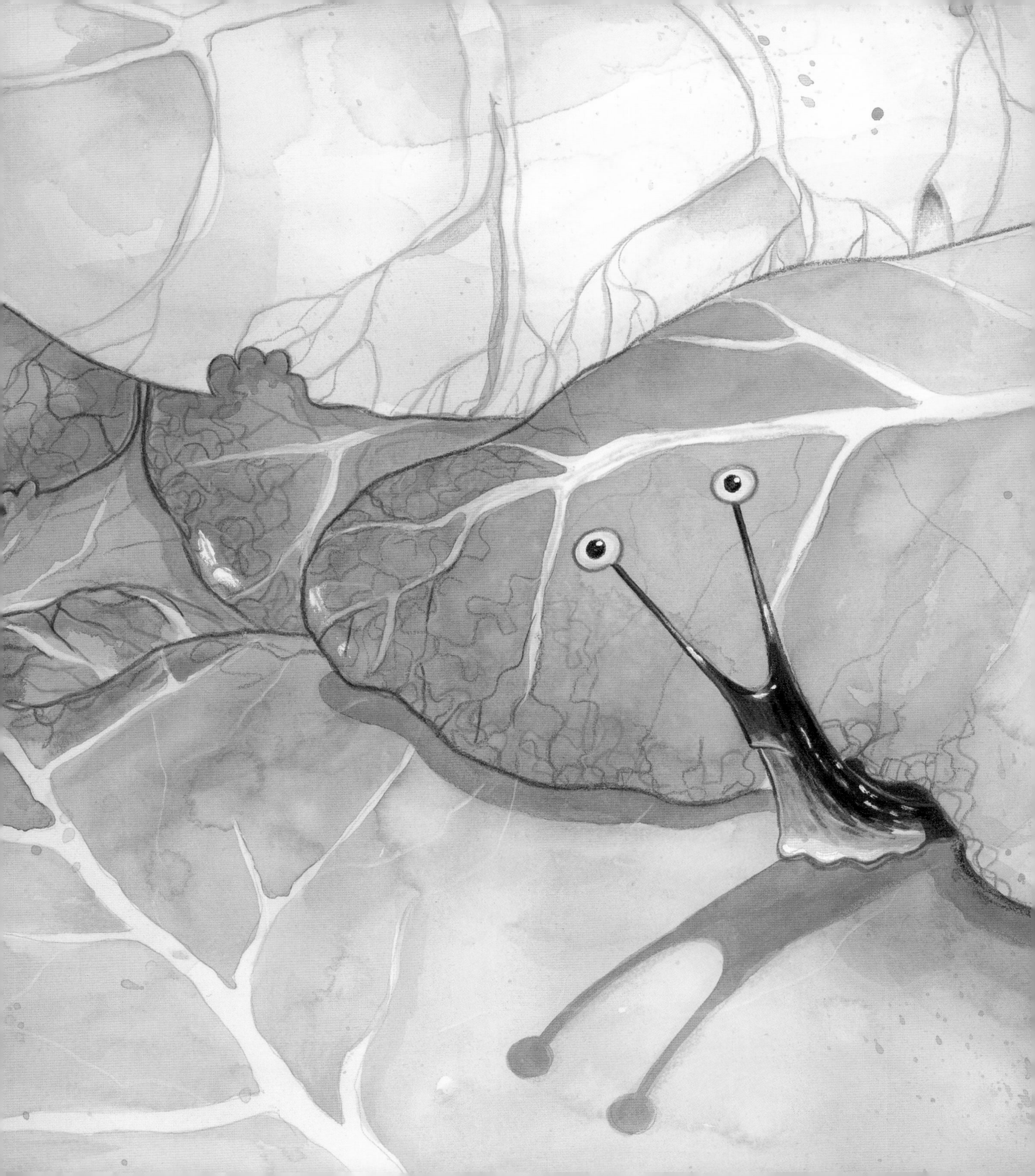

The Biggest, Baddest Wolf

by
Nick Ward

"I am the GREATEST!"

howled Harum Scarum, admiring himself in the mirror as he brushed his fangs. "I am the biggest, baddest, hairiest, scariest wolf in the city!"

white fang

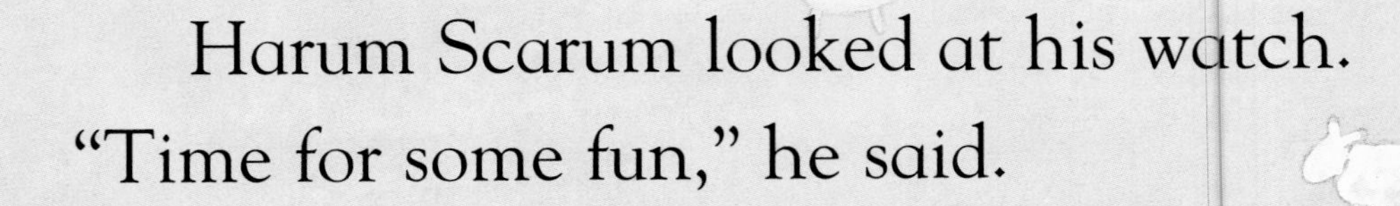

Harum Scarum looked at his watch. "Time for some fun," he said.

Harum Scarum's idea of fun was to scare people. Well, he was the biggest, baddest, hairiest, scariest wolf in the city!

"Do I have everything?" he wondered, patting his pockets. "Money, candy, Teddy . . . Oops, where's my teddy bear?"

Nobody knew that Harum Scarum had a teddy bear, and that he couldn't go anywhere without him.

"Ah! There you are!" he sighed, giving Teddy a big, wet, wolfy kiss.

He put Teddy in his back pocket and went off happily.

The first stop was the park, where Harum Scarum had some fun scaring all the children playing on the swings.

"Run, little children, run, or I'll eat you up!"

he howled.

"Eeek!" they screamed, and rushed away.

"I am the biggest, baddest, hairiest, scariest wolf in the city!" he called after them.

Harum Scarum moved on to the bus stop, where a group of elderly people were waiting.

"Run, old people, run, or I'll eat you up!"

he howled.

"Eeek!" they screamed,
and tottered all the way home.

"I am the biggest, baddest, hairiest, scariest wolf in the city!" he called after them.

For the rest of the day, Harum Scarum worked very hard at scaring anyone he could. He startled a skateboarder . . .

he petrified a builder . . .

and he made a street juggler jump.

"This is fantastic fun!" he cried.

By the time he got home, he was so tired he decided to go straight to bed. And that's when he discovered . . . he'd lost his teddy bear!

"**Oh, no!**" he said, frantically searching his room. He looked here and there . . . but he couldn't find Teddy anywhere.

Harum Scarum crawled sadly into bed. He tossed and turned, but he couldn't get to sleep without his teddy bear to hug.

The next morning, Harum Scarum was a nervous wreck. "I have to find my teddy bear," he wailed, and hurried outside without even brushing his fangs.

He paced the streets. He searched every alleyway. He looked high . . .

and low . . .

But Teddy was nowhere to be seen.

Finally, he arrived at the bus stop.

"Excuse me, have you seen a teddy bear?" he asked the elderly people.

But as soon as they saw him, they tottered all the way home shouting, “Help, it’s the biggest, baddest, hairiest, scariest wolf in the city!”

Harum Scarum went to the park. “Excuse me,” he began, but the little children all rushed off shouting, “Help, it’s the biggest, baddest, hairiest, scariest wolf in the city!”

Harum Scarum sighed, and a tear rolled down his cheek. But just then he noticed one little boy playing on his own. And he was playing with . . . Harum Scarum's teddy bear!

"My teddy bear!" gasped Harum Scarum.

"MY teddy bear!" said the little boy. "Finders keepers."

"Please give him back," Harum Scarum whimpered. "I'm the biggest, baddest, hairiest, scariest wolf in the city."

"You don't look so scary to me," said the little boy.

"Please!" cried Harum Scarum. "I'd do anything to get Teddy back."

"Do you promise to do exactly what you're told from now on?" the little boy said, smiling.

"Of course," he replied.

The very next morning, after a good night's sleep, Harum Scarum brushed his fangs and patted his pockets. Whistling happily, he left home and went straight to the park.

"Hurry up," cried the little children. "We're on the swings! Come and push us."

"Coming," smiled Harum Scarum. He trotted up to the children . . . .

"Run, little children, run, or I'll eat you up!"

"Eeek!" cried the children, rushing off. "You promised!"

"Well, what did you expect?" chuckled Harum Scarum, hugging his teddy bear. "You should NEVER trust the biggest, baddest, hairiest, scariest wolf in the city!"

Bored Bill

by Liz Pichon

Bill was bored. He wasn't just a little bit bored, he was REALLY, REALLY bored.

Bored bored bored . . .

Bill's owner, Mrs. Pickle, was never bored.
She liked to keep busy ALL day.

Mrs. Pickle loved reading, but Bill thought reading was boring.

Mrs. Pickle adored gardening. Bill thought gardening was very dull indeed.

Mrs. Pickle was a fantastic cook and a kung fu expert.

"Try this, Bill, it's fun!!" she said happily.

"Oh, no," sighed Bill.

Mrs. Pickle also liked to do lots of cleaning.

"I'm so bored I can't even move," sighed Bill.

"Come along, Bill, let's go for a nice long walk," Mrs. Pickle said.

"Borrrrrring," muttered Bill.

"Boring dogs get bored," said Mrs. Pickle. "Besides, it's no fun sitting around all day doing nothing."

"I won't go," said Bill firmly.

Outside, the weather was dreadful. It was cold and windy. It was so windy that Mrs. Pickle's hat flew off.

"Whooooops!" Mrs. Pickle laughed.

"How borrring," groaned Bill.

Suddenly, a huge gust of wind swept down and lifted them both off their feet.

"YIPPEEEE!" squealed Mrs. Pickle as she disappeared from sight. Bill clung to a tree when SNAP! the branch broke and he was spun up into the air.

Higher and higher he went. Faster and faster, past the moon and stars

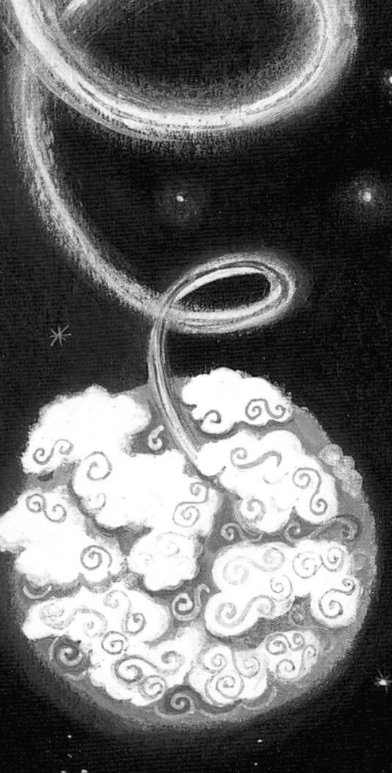

and up into space he flew.

“AT LAST!” cheered Bill.
“No more boring walks for me.
Space will be REALLY exciting.”

THUMP!

Bill landed
on a strange
purple planet.

The noise woke up the aliens. They all popped up to see what it was. Bill was delighted to meet them.

"This planet looks like fun," he smiled. "I bet Mrs. Pickle isn't having an adventure like this!"

Meanwhile, back on EARTH, Mrs. Pickle gets rescued . . . .

Bill asked the aliens to show him the whole planet. "LET'S EXPLORE AND HAVE FUN!" Bill shouted.

"What's the point of exploring?" the aliens sighed. "Exploring is borrrring."

"I'm hungry," one alien mumbled. So they all went to have some squishy green food.

Fantastic! thought Bill. "Alien food MUST be delicious."

But it wasn't. The squishy green food was REVOLTING! Worse still, the aliens ate it for every single meal.

Life on the planet with the aliens was not very interesting at all. They just sat around all day long doing absolutely

NOTHING.

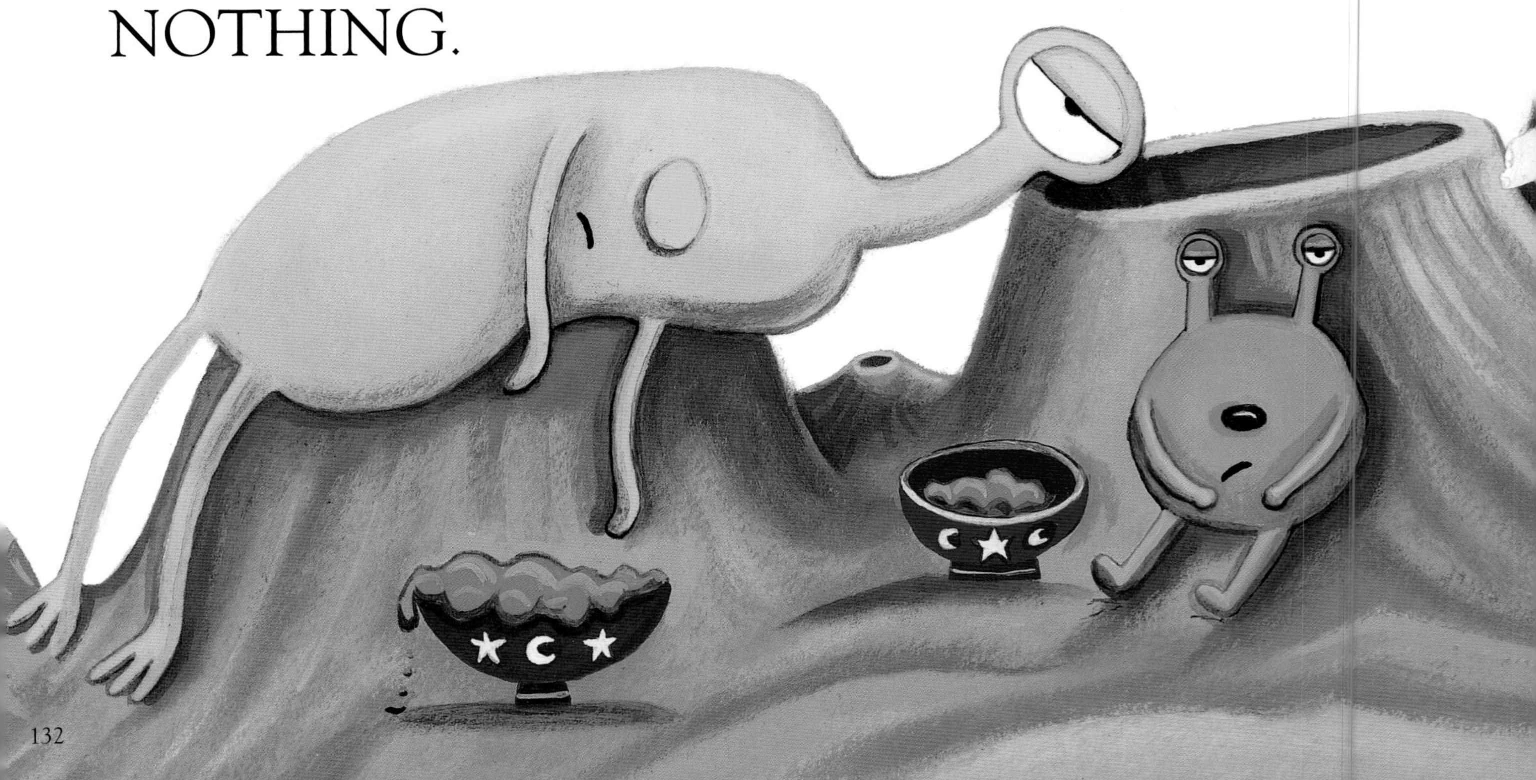

Bill had never been so bored. He really missed Mrs. Pickle and her delicious food.

Bill looked at the aliens lying around the planet. *Mrs. Pickle was right!* he thought suddenly. *Doing nothing all day is REALLY BORING! We need to get BUSY.*

"Come on!" Bill shouted to the aliens. "Boring aliens get bored. It's time to have some fun!"

Bill cooked the aliens a wonderful meal, just like Mrs. Pickle's.

He showed them some of Mrs. Pickle's top kung fu moves.

Then they played some games, which everyone enjoyed.

NOBODY was bored anymore.
But Bill still missed Mrs. Pickle.
He wanted to go home.

So the aliens brought out their spaceship and flew Bill back down to earth. They all waved and said good-bye.

When Bill landed, he found he was FAMOUS!

EVERYONE wanted to talk to Bill about the aliens. But the only person Bill wanted to see was . . .

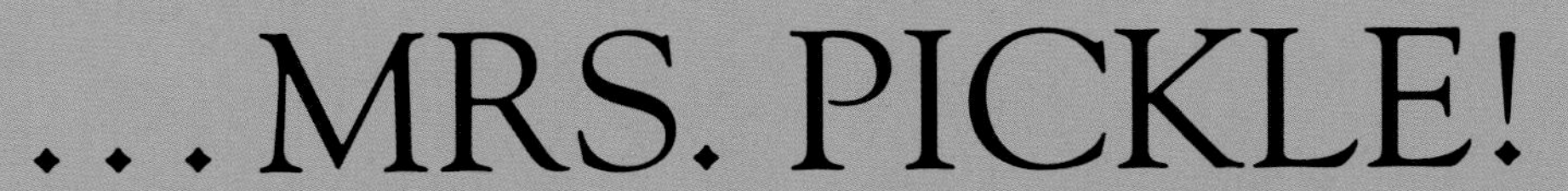

. . . MRS. PICKLE!

"I'll never be bored again!" said Bill as he hugged Mrs. Pickle.

So from that day on, Bill always kept himself busy, just like Mrs. Pickle did. He read books and practiced kung fu.

He dug in the garden and cooked delicious food.

Bill even enjoyed doing the cleaning, which Mrs. Pickle thought was very helpful . . .

Thank you.
Delicious!

. . . especially when they
had so many new friends
around for a party!

I'm Special, I'm Me!

by Ann Meek Illustrated by Sarah Massini

Milo looked in the mirror and sighed a big sigh.

"Come on, Milo, we're going to be late!" Mom called up the stairs.

Milo pressed his nose right up against the cool glass. "What am I going to be today?" he whispered to himself.

At school Milo and his friends were playing a jungle game.

"Please can I be the lion?" asked Milo.

"No," said Claire. "You're not strong enough to be king of the jungle."

So Milo was a sort of sad monkey.

When he got home, Milo peered into the mirror.

"Who can you see?" asked Mom.

"A monkey," replied Milo quietly.

"Lucky you," said Mom. "How fantastic to be able to swing through the trees with all your monkey friends."

"Oh, yeah!" said Milo, grinning and making monkey faces at his mom.

The next day the children were playing a pirate game.

"Please can I be the captain?" asked Milo.

"No," said Ben. "You're too short. The captain has to be tall."

So Milo had to be a deck hand.

“What’s wrong?” asked Mom that evening.

“I wish I were tall, like a pirate captain,” said Milo.

“I think you are just perfect,” said Mom. “Just right for climbing to the top of the sails to be the lookout.”

“Wow!” said Milo, smiling. “I never thought of that.”

The next day, the children were playing prince and princess games.

"Please can I be a prince?" asked Milo.

"No," said Jason. "The prince is handsome like me."

So Milo was an unhappy knight.

Later that afternoon, Milo gazed into the mirror.

"Hello there, Milo," said Mom. "Who can you see looking back at you?"

"I can see a knight," said Milo.

"Terrific!" said Mom. "All that shining armor, and you must be brave because only the bravest men are chosen to be knights, you know."

"Really?" said Milo, a little surprised.

"Definitely," said Mom.

"Cool!" said Milo, pretending to fight a dragon.

The next day, the children were playing spacemen and alien games.

"I'd like to be an astronaut," said Milo, excited.

"No!" said Eloise. "Astronauts can't wear glasses because their helmets wouldn't fit."

So Milo was a little green alien.

Back home, Milo gazed at his reflection in the mirror.

"Do I look like an alien?" he asked.

"You look just like you," said Mom. "Two eyes, a nose, and a mouth, but different from everyone else and that's what makes you special, that's what makes you my Milo." Mom put her arms around him. "And anyway, aliens are so lucky to be able to bounce around in space speaking a secret alien language."

"That's true," Milo smiled. "*Bling, bling, yook, yook,*" he said, bouncing around his bedroom, trying to catch his mom.

The next day, the children were playing an underwater game.

"I'm going to be a shark," said Alex.

"I know what I'm going to be!" said Milo. "I think I'd be a good stingray, hiding in the sand and swimming out and surprising people and making them JUMP!"

The children all stared at Milo . . . .

"Great idea," said Ben.
"Amazing!" said Claire.
"Can I be one, too?" asked Alex.

Milo smiled from ear to ear, and ALL the children pretended to be stingrays under the sea for the rest of the day.

“That was a great game, Milo,” said Ben. “Let’s play it again tomorrow.”

Milo smiled the shiniest smile he had ever smiled.

When he got home that day, Milo looked carefully into his mirror to see if he had changed in any way, but of course he hadn't.

"Mom was right," he said. "I can be whatever I want to be—I'm ME!"

And in the mirror Milo's reflection looked back with a huge, shiny smile!

STORIES FOR BOYS

tiger tales
5 River Road, Suite 128, Wilton, CT 06897
Published in the United States 2015
First published in Great Britain 2015
by Little Tiger Press

ISBN-13: 978-1-58925-535-7
ISBN-10: 1-58925-535-6
Printed in China • LTP/1800/0980/0914

10 9 8 7 6 5 4 3 2 1

For more insight and activities,
visit us at www.tigertalesbooks.com

I'M NOT GOING OUT THERE!

by Paul Bright
Illustrated by Ben Cort

First published in Great Britain 2006
by Little Tiger Press

ROBOT DOG

by Mark Oliver

First published in Great Britain 2005
by Little Tiger Press

DON'T SAY THAT, WILLY NILLY!

by Anna Powell
Illustrated by David Roberts

First published in Great Britain 2005
by Little Tiger Press

THE BIGGEST, BADDEST WOLF

by Nick Ward

First published in Great Britain 2005
by Little Tiger Press

BORED BILL

by Liz Pichon

First published in Great Britain 2005
by Little Tiger Press

I'M SPECIAL, I'M ME!

by Ann Meek
Illustrated by Sarah Massini

First published in Great Britain 2005
by Little Tiger Press